Little Fingers
Make
Nursery
Rhymes

Ten very easy crafts for toddlers

by Marie Thom
and Elizabeth Walton

Illustrated by Olivia Rayner

RAGGED BEARS

Your toddler will love Little Fingers craft activities, and so will you!

Make the nursery rhyme world come to life!

Little Fingers Make Nursery Rhymes is the first in a unique series of books designed specifically for toddlers to build their very own crafts with the minimum of fuss and maximum of enjoyment.

We all know that gluing, sticking and colouring are great fun and do not necessarily need a purpose. However, the craft activities in this book channel these skills into a finished product and, very importantly, give your toddler a new and very individual relationship with much loved nursery rhymes.

Beautifully illustrated and with very simple instructions, all you have to do is cut out the shapes and then get your toddler creating their very own interpretation of their favourite nursery rhyme.

In addition, **Little Fingers** craft activities have a wealth of educational benefits for your toddler.

Each craft :

- develops hand/eye co-ordination, spatial awareness and fine motor skills.

- encourages the following of simple directions and seeing something through to completion.

- introduces colour recognition, counting skills and working with different textures and media.

- gives your child a sense of achievement. The finished product may not look like Humpty Dumpty to you, but to your toddler that's exactly who it is!

All of the activities in these books have been road tested by a large group of toddlers ranging in age from 18 months to 4 years and their grown-ups.

This book is to be returned on or before
the last date stamped below.

		LIBREX

Education

Library Service

CLASS NO:

To Doug, Alistair and Stewart - MT
To Alan, Maddie and Aidan - EW
To Eva and Iris - OR

About the authors: Marie Thom and Elizabeth Walton met at a local toddler group whilst on career breaks from teaching. Before long they were running the group and had initiated a weekly craft activity which proved incredibly popular. Having searched without success for craft books suitable for this age group, they decided to write their own series!

First published in the United Kingdom in 2005 by Ragged Bears Publishing Limited, Milborne Wick, Sherborne, Dorset DT9 4PW
www.raggedbears.co.uk

Distributed by Ragged Bears Limited, Nightingale House, Queen Camel, Somerset BA22 7NN. Tel: 01935 851590

A CIP record of this book is available from the British Library

ISBN HB 1 85714 331 0

PB 1 85714 332 9

Printed in China

You will need:

- Card:
  - gold or yellow
  - silver
- Coloured:
  - paper
  - crepe paper
  - gummed paper
  - tissue paper
- Cotton wool
- Gummed shapes (optional)
- Silver kitchen foil
- Non-toxic glue
- Scissors (for adult to cut out shapes)
- Washable black felt-tip or crayon

A word to the adult!

There's nothing difficult about sourcing any of the materials needed in this book. You should be able to get everything from your local supermarket or stationer.

All the crafts, when done with children under the age of three, must be carried out under adult supervision. Special care should be taken when using sharp equipment, and with small objects that may cause choking. All crafts will require a small amount of adult input before the child can begin: e.g. cutting out shapes and cutting up crepe/tissue paper. You certainly don't have to be an artist to do these crafts. All the shapes are simple and straightforward to copy, draw and cut out and you don't need to be too precise in the way you do it!

Little Fingers crafts can be enjoyed by older children as well. We have included extension activities for the pre-school child (3-5 years old) which require some additional materials:

- Glitter
- Pom-poms
- Wool

Other books in the series: Little Fingers Make Fairy Tales

Sarah, mother of Hannah (aged 2 years 10 months) said, 'Hannah loved doing the crafts after we'd read the nursery rhymes and fairy tales. The activities really made the stories and rhymes come to life for her!'

Lisa, mother of Matthew (aged 3) said, 'Keeping the attention of a three year old is very difficult. These crafts are something fun that we can do together – they keep Matthew entertained and make him feel like he's really done something to be proud of.'

Think of the enjoyment you and your toddler will have together as you read and make each nursery rhyme! There's no mess involved – just lots of fun!

Examples of work done by a group of toddlers.

Crown from
Old King Cole
by Stewart,
aged 2 years
2 months.

*Stewart said,
'Got bits on.'*

Pig from This Little
Piggy by Maddie,
aged 3 years
4 months.

*Maddie said,
'My piggy has a
curly tail – I made it!'*

Candle from Wee
Willie Winkie by
Aidan, aged 2^1/$_2$.

Aidan said,
'It is a candle.'

Fish from One,
Two, Three, Four,
Five by Alistair,
aged 1 year
11 months.

Alistair said,
'Wishy fish.'

Get those little fingers working!

1,2,3,4,5

1,2,3,4,5…Once I caught a fish alive.
6,7,8,9,10…Then I let it go again.
Why did you let it go?
Because it bit my finger so!
Which finger did it bite?
This little finger on my right.

**Ouch! That must have hurt.
Why don't we make a fish
that can't bite?**

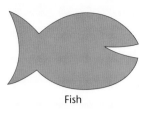

Fish

Scale x5 approx

Bubble x3 approx

What you need

- Blue background paper
- Orange paper
- Blue and orange gummed paper
- Black felt-tip or crayon
- Glue and scissors
- A grown-up to help you do the cutting out. Use the shapes opposite to guide you.

How to do it

- First, cut out the fish shape from orange paper. Cut out scales from orange gummed paper and bubbles from the blue gummed paper.

Now look at the picture below. Are you ready to make your very own fish?

- Stick the fish on to the background paper.
- Stick the scales on to the fish.
- Stick bubbles coming out of the fish's mouth.
- Finish off your fish by drawing in an eye.

Suggestions for older children:

- Add seaweed using green wool.
- Add glitter to the fish.

Hey Diddle Diddle

Hey diddle diddle,
The cat and the fiddle,
The cow jumped over the moon.
The little dog laughed,
To see such fun,
And the dish ran away with the spoon.

**This lovely cow is for you to make
– stick it down quickly before it jumps off the page!**

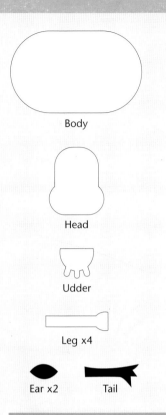

Body

Head

Udder

Leg x4

Ear x2   Tail

What you need

- Background paper
  – any colour you want
- White paper
- Black crepe paper (cut into pieces)
- Black paper

- Black felt-tip or crayon
- Glue and scissors
- A grown-up to help you do the cutting out. Use the shapes opposite to guide you.

How to do it

- Cut out the body, head, udder and legs from white paper.
  Cut out the tail and ears from black paper.

Now look at the picture below. Are you ready to make your very own cow?

- Stick the cow's body on to the background paper.
- Stick the head, udder, legs, tail and ears to the body.
- Decorate cow with black crepe paper.
- Finish off your cow by drawing in a face.

Suggestions for older children:

- Use plaited wool for tail.
- Stick scrunched-up pieces of pink tissue to the ears and udder.

Little Miss Muffet

Little Miss Muffet,
Sat on her tuffet,
Eating her curds and whey.
There came a big spider
Who sat down beside her
And frightened Miss Muffet away.

Can you make this very friendly spider?
Don't run away from it!

Body

Leg x8

Eye x2

What you need

- Black paper or card
- Yellow gummed paper
- Black felt-tip or crayon
- Glue and scissors
- A grown-up to help you do the cutting out.
  Use the shapes opposite to guide you.

How to do it

- Cut out the spider and eight legs from black paper. Cut out two circles from yellow gummed paper.

Now look at the picture below. Are you ready to make your very own spider?

- Stick legs on to the body and eyes on to the head.
- Finish your spider off by drawing in the centre of the eyes.

Suggestions for older children:

- Use black wool instead of paper for the legs.
- Add a wool loop to spider's head and hang it up.

This Little Piggy

This little piggy went to market,
This little piggy stayed at home,
This little piggy had roast beef,
And this little piggy had none,
And this little piggy went, 'Wee, wee, wee!'
All the way home.

Those little darlings get everywhere! Can you make this cute little piggy before it runs all the way home?

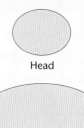

Head

Body

Ear x2

Leg x4

Tail

What you need

- Background paper
  – any colour you want
- Pink paper
- Piece of pink tissue paper
- Black felt-tip or crayon

- Glue and scissors
- A grown-up to help you do the cutting out. Use the shapes opposite to guide you.

How to do it

- First cut out legs, head, body and ears from pink paper. Then cut out a long strip from pink paper for tail and wrap the strip tightly around a pencil to make the tail curl.

Now look at the picture below. Are you ready to make your very own pink piggy?

- Stick the pig's body on to the background paper.
- Stick the legs, head and tail to body; stick the ears to the head.
- Scrunch up piece of pink tissue and stick on for nose.
- Finish your pig off by drawing on two eyes and a mouth.

Suggestions for older children:

- Use pink or white wool to make a curly tail.

Humpty Dumpty

Humpty Dumpty sat on a wall
Humpty Dumpty had a great fall
All the King's horses
And all the King's men
Couldn't put Humpty together again.

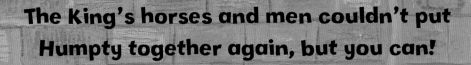

**The King's horses and men couldn't put
Humpty together again, but you can!**

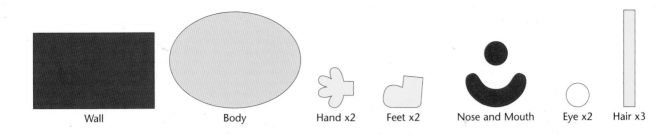

Wall   Body   Hand x2   Feet x2   Nose and Mouth   Eye x2   Hair x3

What you need

- Background paper
  – any colour you want
- Brown, beige, yellow, red
  and white paper
- Brown crepe paper (cut into pieces)
- Black felt-tip or crayon
- Glue and scissors
- A grown-up to help you do the
  cutting out. Use the shapes above
  to guide you.

How to do it

- First, cut out the wall from brown
  paper. Next, cut out the body from
  beige paper. Now cut out hands and
  feet from yellow paper and the mouth
  and nose from red paper. Cut out eye
  shapes from white paper. Lastly, cut out
  three strips of hair from yellow paper
  and wrap around a pencil to make
  them curl.

**Now look at the picture opposite.
Are you ready to make your
very own Humpty on a wall?**

- Stick the wall at the bottom of the
  background paper.
- Stick Humpty's body on to the wall.
- Stick on the hands, feet, hair and face.
- Cover the wall with brown crepe paper.
- Finish off your Humpty by drawing in
  the centre of the eyes.

Suggestions for older children:

- Use wool for hair.

Old King Cole

Old King Cole was a merry old soul
And a merry old soul was he.
He called for his pipe
And he called for his drum
And he called for his fiddlers three.

He's a very jolly king isn't he?
Why don't you make a crown fit for a king or queen?

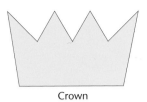

Crown

What you need

- Gold or yellow card
- Cotton wool
- Tissue paper (torn into pieces)
- Gummed paper or gummed shapes
- Glue
- Scissors
- A grown-up to help you do the cutting out. Use the shape opposite to guide you.

How to do it

- First cut out the crown from gold or yellow card. Cut out little jewel-like shapes from the gummed paper.

Now look at the picture below. Are you ready to make your very own crown?

- Stick cotton wool along the bottom of the crown.
- Scrunch up pieces of tissue paper and stick them to the crown points.
- Decorate the crown with gummed paper shapes.

Suggestions for older children:

- Use pompoms instead of tissue paper on the crown points.
- Sprinkle glitter on the crown.

Baa Baa Black Sheep

Baa baa black sheep have you any wool?
Yes sir! Yes sir! Three bags full.
One for the master,
And one for the dame,
And one for the little boy,
Who lives down the lane.

What a lot of wool!
Here is a cuddly sheep for you to make.

Body

Face

Leg x4

Eye x2

Nose

What you need

- Background paper
  – any colour you want
- Black and white paper
- Black crepe paper (cut into pieces)
- Black felt-tip or crayon

- Glue and scissors
- A grown-up to help you do the cutting out. Use the shapes opposite to guide you.

How to do it

- Cut out the sheep's body, face and four legs from black paper. Then cut out two eyes and a nose from white paper.

Now look at the picture below. Are you ready to make your very own baa baa black sheep?

- Stick the sheep's body on to the background paper.
- Stick the head and legs to the body.
- Stick the eyes and nose to the head.
- Cover the sheep's body with black crepe paper.
- Scrunch up pieces of black crepe paper and stick them on for the tail. Now finish your sheep off, by drawing in the centre of the eyes.

Suggestions for older children:

- Use black wool instead of crepe paper to cover the sheep.

Sing a Song of Sixpence

Sing a song of sixpence, a pocket full of rye.
Four and twenty blackbirds baked in a pie.
When the pie was opened
The birds began to sing.
Wasn't that a dainty dish
To set before the King?

That's a very strange filling for a pie! You can make a 'bird pie' too – with just two birds instead of 24!

Pie Lid

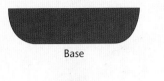

Base

Blackbird x2

Beak x2

Eye x4

What you need

- Background paper
  – any colour you want
- Brown paper
- Brown crepe paper (cut into pieces)
- Black felt-tip or crayon

- Glue and scissors
- A grown-up to help you do the cutting out. Use the shapes opposite to guide you.

How to do it

- First, cut out the pie base and lid from brown paper. Using the coloured gummed paper cut out two blackbirds from the black, two beaks from the orange and four eyes from the yellow.

Now look at the picture below. Are you ready to make your very own blackbird pie?

- Stick the pie base and lid on to the background paper.
- Stick the blackbirds into the pie.
- Stick the eyes and beaks on to the birds.
- Draw in the centre of the eyes.
- Finish the pie off by covering it with the pieces of brown crepe paper.

Suggestions for older children:

- Add scrunched up pieces of black tissue paper to the birds.

Wee Willie Winkie

Wee Willie Winkie runs through the town,
Upstairs and downstairs in his night gown.
Knocking at the windows,
Crying through the locks,
'Are the children in their beds?
It's past eight o'clock.'

Wee Willie Winkie carried a candle to light his way.
How bright will the flame be on your candle?

Candle-dish

Handle

Candle

Flame

What you need

- Background paper
  – any colour you want
- Black, white and red paper
- Red and yellow tissue paper
  (cut into pieces)
- Black felt-tip or crayon
- Glue and scissors
- A grown-up to help you do
  the cutting out. Use the
  shapes above to guide you.

How to do it

- First cut out the candle-dish
  and handle from black paper.
  Cut out the candle from white
  paper. Then cut out the flame
  from red paper.

**Now look at the picture
opposite. Are you ready to
make your very own candle?**

- Stick the candle, dish
  and handle on to the
  background paper.
- Draw a wick and stick the
  flame on to it.
- Finish your candle off by
  covering the flame with
  scrunched up red and
  yellow tissue paper.

Suggestions for older children:

- Decorate candle dish with glitter.
- Cover candle in pieces of white crepe paper.

Twinkle, Twinkle

Twinkle, Twinkle little star

How I wonder what you are.

Up above the world so high,

Like a diamond in the sky.

Twinkle, twinkle, little star

How I wonder what you are.

The stars in the sky seem so far away.
Here are some you can make and keep close to you.

Triangle x6

Strip

What you need

- Black paper
- Gold or silver or yellow card
- Glue and scissors
- A grown-up to help you do the cutting out.
  Use the shapes opposite to guide you.

How to do it

- Cut out six triangles from the gold, silver or yellow card.
- Cut out a strip of black paper.

Now look at the picture below. Are you ready to make your very own twinkling stars?

- To make each star stick one triangle on top of another.
- Finish your stars off by sticking them to the black strip of paper.

Suggestions for older children:

- Use wool instead of paper to connect the stars.
- Decorate the stars with glitter.